Copyright © 2023, Kyle Andrews. All rights reserved.

This book, or parts thereof, may not be reproduced in any form without written permission of the author, except in the case of brief quotations used in critical articles or reviews.

ISBN: 9798851934506

This is a work of fiction. Names, characters, places, businesses and incidents are either the product of the author's imagination or are used fictitiously. Any resemblance to actual persons, living or dead, businesses, events or locales is purely coincidental.

For Emma
Because she did too.

She Danced

A NOVELLA BY
KYLE ANDREWS

Maureen Whitlock was born somewhere in Nebraska, in the year 1943. She didn't know where she was born exactly, because her mother never told her such things. That was the past, and as far as her mother was concerned, the past was nothing worth remembering. The past was where the pain lived. The past was where Maureen's father died.

Like many other children of her generation, Maureen had lost her father in the war. Her mother never told her much more than that, so all Maureen knew of the man was what she had made up herself.

Her daddy was a hero. That was the thing she knew the most, above all else. He had probably died charging into battle, to save a train full of small children and sick old people from being killed by the bad guys.

As her daddy fought that battle, he saw an evil man taking aim at a little girl, who reminded him of the daughter that he'd never met back home.

Unable to bear seeing that little girl hurt in any way, Maureen's father placed himself between the evil man and that other little girl, and he took the bullet for her.

As the little girl cried and cradled Maureen's father in her little arms, he looked into her eyes and told her to let his daughter know how much he loved her, and how he would be with her always.

That was when he died.

Maureen always cried at the thought of his death when she was a little girl, because to her, his death marked a turning point. After that moment, she wasn't just a little girl, living a normal life. She was her mother's coping mechanism. It was her job to make things better.

After becoming a widow at the ripe old age of twenty-three, Maureen's mother was shattered. Up until that point, she'd known what her life was supposed to be. She was supposed to be the wife of a war hero, and the mother to his children. She was supposed to help out at church picnics, and organize class trips for the elementary school.

She was supposed to be what *her* mother had always been, but what her mother had never been was alone.

Now, Maureen's mother had a child to feed. She needed to afford clothing for the both of them, and somewhere for them to

SHE DANCED

live. She needed to pay for doctor bills, and figure out all of the paperwork that came with living a normal life.

She hated it. She resented both Maureen for being born, and Maureen's father for dying. Oh, she loved both of them too, but she hated the position that she'd been put in because of them, and she wasn't sure what she was supposed to do next.

Then there was a silly comment, made by a silly woman at one of their church gatherings. The woman looked down at little Maureen, who was barely old enough to stand on her own two feet, and she told her mother that the child was a doll, beautiful enough to be a star on the big screen. Why, she could be the next Shirley Temple.

That was when the thought was first placed into the head of Maureen's mother. After that, she couldn't look at the child without wondering why she couldn't be the next Shirley Temple. Sure, there were other cute children in the world, but her Maureen was just as cute as any of them. There was no reason why it couldn't have worked.

The thought festered like an ugly wound inside of her for the next couple of years. It wasn't that this was a good plan for the future. It simply *was* a plan. It was a direction to point herself in, and a target to aim for.

If there was one thing that Maureen's mother had never been good at, it was wandering aimlessly through life. Once she had a goal set, she was like a torpedo, blasting through anything that got in her way.

Despite the protests of Maureen's grandparents, Maureen's mother packed up as much of their things as would fit into their rusty old car, and when Maureen was three years old, she and her mother left their home for California.

Los Angeles.

Hollywood.

That world would become all that Maureen would know as a child. She would never be just a girl, going to school and playing with her friends. She would be the girl who had to take singing lessons, followed by dancing lessons, while socializing with all of the other girls who were there to do the exact same thing as her.

Every sleepover was a game of sizing up the competition, but Maureen hated that. She wanted to see her friends succeed, and she never wanted to hope for them to fail, even if it meant that she herself failed in the process.

Her mother kept telling her to work harder and do better, and not to see it as taking something from someone else. She told Maureen to look at it as the chance to take something that was meant for her.

But Maureen wasn't so sure.

Oh, she could sing as well as anyone, she supposed. And she could act too. She could cry on command, without even needing to take the time to make herself feel bad.

The one thing she couldn't do was dance. No matter how many lessons she took, or how hard she tried, she could never get

SHE DANCED

her body to move the way her teacher wanted it to. She could never glide across the stage as gracefully as the other girls.

Shirley Temple could dance.

If Maureen couldn't do that one simple thing, she would never be the next Shirley Temple, and that would mean that her mother had given up everything she had ever known, in order to pursue a dream that would never become a reality.

Maureen's mother wasn't one of those mothers who would beat her child for failing to land a part. She didn't drink, or do any of the really horrible things that some of the other parents did to their children. Her mother was just sad. And when her mother was sad, she would let Maureen know that she was sad, and she would also let the girl know that everything depended on Maureen making it as an actress.

In those early years, Maureen's mother worked as a waitress in a diner, down the street from their apartment. She also had jobs in department stores, a drug store, and once spent a week trying to be a secretary for a cheap lawyer.

Her mother worked hard, just for the sake of giving Maureen the best chance she could have at making something of her life, and Maureen loved her mother for it.

But Maureen had a secret. It was something that she never dared to speak aloud, and certainly not in front of her mother. It was the one thing that she feared would get her a smack right across the face, even if her mother had never threatened to do it.

Her secret was, she didn't really want to be an actress. After years of growing up in that place, and learning all of the things that she needed to learn in order to become one, Maureen didn't enjoy any of it.

While most of the children she knew went to sleep, dreaming about winning that breakout role and seeing themselves up there on the big screen, Maureen went to sleep at night telling herself stories of a normal girl, running through a field with her friends. A girl playing hopscotch on the sidewalk. A girl who could scrape her knee without her mother worrying that it would cost her the next audition.

She'd seen it in the movies. She'd heard her mother telling countless stories about what life was like when she was a little girl, and how she had grown up with Maureen's daddy, catching frogs near some old pond.

Maureen had never experienced anything like that for herself, however. It was as much a fantasy to her as Hollywood was to anyone else.

∞

Everyone's end is a sad one. At least, that's the way people act. No matter what you do with your life, or how old you are when you die, the people who are left behind always talk about what a shame it is that you're gone. Even if they don't know you

SHE DANCED

at all, they'll shake their head and put on a mournful expression, just because it's the thing to do.

Maureen Danvers was dying. She'd been dying for so long that nobody could claim to be surprised by the news when it finally happened.

It was 2017 now, and Maureen was 74 years old. A strange age for her to be, in her mind. Old enough to feel old, but younger than she'd always imagined she would be when she died.

Somehow, she'd always pictured herself as one of those extremely stubborn women, still living in her own house and driving her own car when she was a century old. She always wanted to be one of those hardcore grandmother's, who said whatever was on her mind, while drinking whiskey and flirting with men who were young enough to be her grandchildren.

She never was that person though. She was too nice, and too proper—the result of a childhood spent learning how to be professional and mature.

It was just as well. The young men who worked in the nursing home where she lived looked like babies to her. The thought of flirting with them was disgusting.

If you had told Maureen ten years earlier that she would be living in a nursing home, waiting to die, she would have told you that you were a fool. She'd have told you to pull the plug when the time came, and hold her funeral on the curb, on trash day.

Here she was though. Lying in bed, listening to the sound of her own struggled breathing, while two of the nurses who worked in the home made conversation, as though she weren't even there.

"Henry said that he wanted to go to Alaska," one of the nurses—Shelly—told the other. "Alaska. Who wants to go to Alaska on a vacation? So, I said that we're either going to Hawaii, or we're not wasting the money. I could use a new washer and dryer anyway."

It wasn't that Maureen lacked the ability to take part in the conversation. At least, she believed that she could still do that if she wanted to. The thing was, she didn't want to. She was content to live in her own little world, listening to other people go on with life as though she were already dead.

The journey to this point was much longer than Maureen would have figured. It started with little choices made as a child, and slightly larger choices made as a young woman. Choices piled on top of choices, which piled on top of choices, and now she was buried beneath a mountain of them.

Then there were genetic factors. Her own mother had died young. Maureen had felt as though she were living on borrowed time ever since she'd passed the age her mother had been when she died.

Of course, her mother had also smoked three packs a day, and died of lung cancer.

SHE DANCED

Maureen herself had a weak heart. She'd suffered three heart attacks before her children eventually decided that she couldn't live by herself anymore. They both lived in other states, and they worried about her being alone.

"I've been to Alaska," Tilly, the other nurse, responded. "You shouldn't rule it out. No tropical beaches, but the views are amazing."

"If I want to see a view of Alaska, I can Google it," Shelly replied.

Beaches were overrated, in Maureen's opinion. She'd grown up near the beach, and it was fun for a while. Then it became annoying. The crowded streets. The loud music. The drinking.

She'd love to see Alaska though.

For a while, after Maureen moved into the home, her kids were there to visit. They were dealing with all of the business of selling her house and holding the estate sale, wherein all of her belongings were sold before she'd even died.

It was morbid, but Maureen didn't mind that. In a way, it was liberating. It was an interesting feeling, to suddenly cut loose all of the little things that she'd collected for herself over so many decades.

For a brief moment, she considered giving them a list of trinkets that she wanted to hold onto. Her mother's silver comb, they might keep and pass on to one of her granddaughters, but other things, like the rock that she'd always kept on her nightstand… would they even think twice about throwing it away? She'd never even told them why she'd put it there.

The thing was, it didn't matter anymore. She wasn't going to that home to live out a long and fruitful life. She was going there to die, and when she did that, the rock would become just a rock once again—just as it had been when it was given to her.

Shelly picked up an old photo of Maureen that was sitting on her bedside table now, and she looked at the young girl that Maureen had once been with a smile.

"Aren't you a looker," she said to Maureen, but Maureen didn't respond.

Maybe she really couldn't talk anymore. She didn't know how long it had been since she'd tried.

Her eyes were open only a sliver. She was so tired. Her body felt as if it weighted a thousand pounds. She felt trapped there, pinned to the bed.

"I just love these old pictures," Shelly said, more to Tilly than to Maureen. "My kids send me selfies. I could never get them to sit down for a real picture like this. They don't even dress up for school pictures anymore. My daughter wanted to wear her pajama pants to school yesterday."

Shelly put the photo down on the table once again, and though Maureen didn't turn to look at the thing, she knew which picture it was.

Her younger son had placed it on the table, not long after the estate sale. He wanted to bring back good memories for her, but Maureen cringed at the thought of looking at her own picture every day.

SHE DANCED

The photo was an old headshot, from when Maureen was sixteen years old. It had taken her ages to get the shot taken, because her best friend had been just off to the side, cracking jokes and making her laugh.

Her mother was furious, but the end result was a picture of young Maureen, looking just off to the side of the camera, in the millisecond just before she burst into laughter.

In her eyes, you can see the joy and lightness, and it lent the headshot a feeling of youthfulness that was usually lacking in over-posed headshots.

She could feel her eyes filling with tears as the memory of that photo shoot came back to her, and the thought of her friend. He'd always known how to bring her out of her own head. He made her better than she ever felt she was.

God, she was tired. She was so incredibly tired, and she wanted to rest, but her mind was racing.

Once she thought about that photo shoot, she thought about everything that came after it. So many days. So many years.

Maureen had been a widow for fifteen years. That thought alone made her head spin.

Bill was a good man. He worked hard. He gave her a life that she never thought she could have, in a place that had once seemed so alien to her.

Her life was a good one. She loved what she had made of it. She loved her children. She loved her friends. It was a small life, perhaps, but it was her whole world.

Her wedding flashed before her eyes.

Birthday parties.

Family vacations.

Filing taxes. Making coffee. Walking the dog, and then the other dog, and another. Music playing on the radio as she vacuumed the house with all of the windows open. The smell of laundry coming through the vent on the side of the house, on a beautiful spring day.

"Have you ever eaten at that new place down the road?" Tilly asked.

"The one that's in the building where the diner used to be?" Shelly replied.

"Yeah."

"Not yet. I was thinking of going sometime."

"Let me know if you do."

Maureen wanted to lift her arm and scratch her nose, but she didn't. She still wasn't sure if she was incapable of moving, or if she was just so tired that she couldn't work up the will to do it.

She'd heard someone say that they'd called her family to let them know that it could be any time now, but she wasn't sure if anyone would come. They'd been through this twice before, and she'd made two miraculous recoveries. Whether or not they were on their way, she was alone now.

Nobody she loved was sitting by her bedside, but that was ok. She loved them. She wanted them to be living their lives, not crying over her. She wanted to imagine them sitting outside,

SHE DANCED

laughing and enjoying a nice meal. She didn't want them to be stuck sitting on a faux leather recliner that squeaked every time you so much as looked at it the wrong way.

Maureen was a private woman. Dying felt like something that she should do on her own. She was fine with it.

She was. Really.

And yet, there was some part of her that was waiting for someone to show up and take her hand. In some way, she felt like she'd been waiting for him to get there forever.

"Maureen," she heard a voice whisper from the doorway.

A young, vibrant, beautiful voice.

She could see someone moving closer, but her vision was blurry. She could see the shape of the young man, but not his face.

Neither Shelly nor Tilly said anything to him as he moved closer to the bed.

Then he was sitting on the mattress beside her, looking down at her.

"Deep breath," he said in a calm tone. "We move on three."

She smiled the biggest smile that she could muster as his face came into focus for the first time. His blue eyes. His perfectly combed hair.

It wasn't much of a smile, really, since she couldn't make her facial muscles respond to her commands, but she was delighted to see him there. Her heart swelled, and she felt light as a feather for the first time in ages.

She took a deep breath, and whispered, "My Mickey."

Maureen had a secret, which nobody in that room knew except for him.

They didn't know who she was, and that was good. She'd always wanted it that way. They could look at that old picture of her, and they didn't know what it meant. They could hear her name—even her maiden name—and it wouldn't mean a thing to any of them.

They were too young. Too much time had passed.

The secret she kept was something that belonged to her alone now. It was a moment in time. It was a feeling of letting go, and being carried on the air itself.

Maureen Danvers died, not surrounded by family, as one always imagined their own death. Her passing was not reported in any headlines, as her mother would have dreamed for her. In truth, there weren't even that many tears shed.

Her secret—the one which she would take with her to her grave—was not something that she had never told anyone. It was something long forgotten, by a great many people.

The secret was, that in her youth, and for just a little while, she danced.

∞

"Your feet are like little blocks of cement, stuck to the ends of two broomsticks, tied to the body of a dead cow."

SHE DANCED

This was the first criticism that Maureen could remember getting from one of her teachers. Oh, there were probably many more before that, but this was the first memory of it that she had managed to retain.

The teacher was Mrs. Thorp, and she looked like the product of a technicolor lab accident. She had bright red hair, with bright pink lips. Deep blue eye shadow, with thick black liner around each eye, and a beauty mark on one of her cheeks. She wore big, ruffled dresses, with splashes of color everywhere she could manage to find room.

When she spoke, Mrs. Thorp had a thick accent, but Maureen couldn't tell if it was German, French or Russian. Maybe she would have been able to tell the difference if she'd started the dialect classes that her mother wanted to put her in, but couldn't afford.

Maureen was five years old when Mrs. Thorp spoke those words to her, and even at that young age, the little girl knew that the woman wasn't wrong.

She would sit in the back of class sometimes, and watch the other little girls practice their ballet, or their ballroom dancing. In her childish mind, they looked like kites, floating on the wind, spinning and diving with each stray gust.

It was beautiful, but no matter how hard she worked at it, the movements just never came to her. Each time she was going to twirl, she would think about what those other girls looked like and how she could never be so graceful, and she would end up tripping over her own feet.

"No, no, no, no, no," her teachers would say; first Mrs. Thorp, then Mr. Linden, then Hines, Winsted, and others whose names she didn't even remember.

As Maureen got older, she began to realize how disappointed her mother looked each time Maureen left class with another one of those comments.

Five years old, and she was already a failure. Her mother wouldn't yell at her or punish her though.

One time, she saw another girl's mother slap the girl across the face for getting one step wrong, but Maureen's mother never did that. She just got quiet, and sad, and Maureen knew that she'd done something bad.

Every one of those other children was out to get the same thing as Maureen. For every one role that the studios held auditions for, there would be a thousand little girls who looked just like Maureen.

Maureen could act, but so could they.

Maureen could sing, but they could too.

Those other girls could dance, however, and that meant that every time Maureen walked into one of those auditions, she was doing so at a disadvantage.

Before she ever learned how to add two plus two, Maureen had learned what it was like to be rejected for countless jobs.

SHE DANCED

If only she could dance... At least, that's what she told herself. Whether or not it was true didn't matter.

This went on for a long time, and eventually her mother came to accept that Maureen would never be a dancer. Instead, she focused on drama classes and vocal coaches. She made sure that Maureen knew how to read as early as possibly, so that she could rehearse scenes without having to be fed her lines.

They didn't have much money, so the two of them lived in a tiny apartment, which barely had any furniture in it at all. They didn't even have a radio. Instead, they would open their window and listen to a radio from one building over, because the man who owned that radio liked to listen to it very loudly.

There was no money for fancy hairdressers, so Maureen's mother would make do with what she had handy. She used old rags to make curlers for both of them, and only wore makeup when she absolutely had to.

Maureen's mother wore clothes that were old, but she'd refashioned them and made them look new enough that while other women might think she had bad taste, they would never suspect that she couldn't afford new clothes.

Whatever money they had was spent on clothes for Maureen. She was the one who would be standing in front of the directors and producers, being judged on how she looked.

Her mother always bought clothes that were just a little bit too big for Maureen, and then altered them to fit, so that she would be able to let out the seams as the child grew.

"Tricks of the trade," her mother would smile as she did this. For her, being the mother of a potential actress was a full-time job of its own.

For a long time, this was the way things went for them. They worked hard, but there was very little reward for their efforts.

Every so often, someone would make a stray comment about how adorable little Maureen was, and her mother would use those compliments to drive her forward, even when things looked hopeless.

By the time Maureen was seven years old, she was beginning to feel like an old has-been. In her mind, her glory days were behind her, though she couldn't think of any specific days that felt glorious.

Her mother was getting more quiet as time passed, and she cried more often than she used to. The need to keep pushing forward had once kept her from thinking about her dead husband, and the life that had been denied her, but as she settled into the routine of poverty and rejection, she started to have doubts about what they were doing out there in California.

It should have been easier. It seemed like such a sure thing when they'd first arrived. Why wasn't it working?

In Maureen's mind, it all tied back to the fact that she couldn't dance. This meant that she wasn't good enough. It was her fault.

She thought this, even though most of the girls she knew could dance, and they were all in the same boat. She'd known one

SHE DANCED

girl who had landed a role in some silly movie, and moved away. Maureen didn't know what happened to her, but it didn't really matter. Everyone else was working hard and earning nothing.

It felt hopeless, but things did eventually change.

Oh, Maureen wasn't signed to a big studio, and she wasn't given the lead role in any major motion pictures. However, when she was seven years old, Maureen stepped foot onto her first movie set.

She was a background player. An extra. It was a thankless job, but it was more than she'd had before, and she did the job well.

In that first movie, she was playing a schoolgirl, walking down hallways and sitting in class, while the movie's lead actress played her drunken teacher.

Nobody even noticed that she was there. While all of the other little kids were trying their best to act adorable and draw attention to themselves, Maureen sat in a dark corner, and watched all of the people who were doing their jobs around her.

It was a dance, she thought. All of those people, moving in different directions, but still in harmony with each other. All moving to create the same final image.

It was a dance, and in some small way, she was a part of it.

She loved being on set, and watching the real actors doing their jobs. She thought it was so funny, how one actress would make herself miserable all day, just so she could cry in one scene.

Maureen could cry, even when she was happy.

Another actor would be laughing and making jokes with the crew, and then turn around and play a dramatic scene as though he'd flipped a switch and turned off the humor.

That movie was just the first that Maureen worked on. Once she was in the system, she was given more chances to work as an extra in other movies. Once the people doing the hiring knew that she could be counted on to do the job without pestering the directors or lead actors, they started calling her mother and asking for her by name. For once, her tendency to blend into the background was working in her favor.

It wasn't what her mother had dreamed of when they'd moved out to California, but it was real work. Maureen was making money for the first time in her six years of life, and it was exciting for both of them.

Maureen wasn't seen on screen in her first movie, despite the hours that she'd spent working on it. Her second movie, however, had her mother screeching in the little movie theater that they were watching it in.

In that movie, Maureen walked right behind one of the main characters, and her face was clearly visible for roughly three tenths of a second, but it was enough to thrill her mother for a week.

She did more movies, and even some television shows. She was always an extra, but she was able to sing in the background of musicals, and scream in the background of monster movies.

One time, she got to sit on a barrel while John Wayne walked by and patted her on the head. Her mother nearly fainted, but the shot was cut from the movie, so you'd never even know that she was there.

The more time that she and her mother spent on those big movie lots, the more they got to know the different crew members who worked there. They became friends with many of them, though there were a few who her mother never seemed to like very much. She'd always yank Maureen away from them when they tried to talk with the young girl.

Eventually, her mother started taking different jobs on the lots, working in the wardrobe department sometimes, or as an assistant to one of the directors.

One of the crew members that they often saw around the different movie sets was Frank Lauden, who was one of the men who helped to build the sets that movies were filmed on.

He was always nice to Maureen, bringing her pieces of candy as an excuse to come over and talk to her mother.

Frank and Maureen's mother started eating lunch together whenever they were working on the same project, and over time, he became a part of their family. He married Maureen's mother when Maureen was nine years old.

Maureen liked Frank. He was nice. Once she and her mother moved into his small house, he became the father that she'd never had before. He would drive her to work when her mother wasn't able to. He would make sure that nobody mistreated her. He even took her horseback riding one weekend, when her mother had to work.

Frank was great, and Maureen loved him, but when her mother sat her down one day, and told her that they were going to be changing their last name, and taking Frank's, Maureen felt traumatized.

All she had ever known of her real father was his name. It was all she shared with him. It was all he was able to give her before he died.

What a strange thing for a little girl to go through. To be told that your own name was going to change because two other people were getting married felt wrong. It felt like a betrayal of her grandparents back home, and her uncle, and her cousins, whom she didn't even know.

The decision was made, however, and on June 12, 1952, Maureen Whitlock was gone forever. After that day, she was Maureen Lauden.

This was the name that she would eventually see on screen. It was how she would be introduced by announcers when her face appeared. It was the reason why success never felt like it belonged to her.

∞

In 2007, Maureen was sixty-four years old. A widow of five years. Mother to two children, both of whom had left home for college years earlier, and never moved back.

SHE DANCED

She was a woman who was still defining herself based on who she was to people who no longer needed her. She had grandkids, and she loved them, but they barely knew her.

Maureen was adrift, in a house that she'd once lived in, but now she just existed there. She would wake up each morning and make coffee, just as she always had. The only difference was that she now dumped half the pot down the drain, because she'd never gotten out of the habit of making enough coffee for two people.

She ate breakfast, not because she was hungry, but because it was what she was supposed to do at that time of day.

In the past, she would have made pancakes or waffles, or fancy omelets with mushrooms and onions. Now she poured a bowl of cereal, and sat down in her quiet kitchen, in her quiet house.

She kept the TV on in the other room, tuned in to one of the cable news networks, which only served to make her feel more isolated and more depressed. The world wasn't getting any better. It seemed like a new war started every week, because the people who ran the country were in just as much of a rut as she was. If they actually solved any of the problems facing this world, they wouldn't know what to do with themselves.

Every day was like this. Sometimes she would hear a lawn mower outside, or a delivery truck driving by, and that was the most excitement she would have for the day.

It was hard to believe that the girl who had started working before she could remember, and who had spent two decades chasing after her boys—the woman who had hosted work parties for her husband and helped to organize the neighborhood watch back in 1986—was now sitting by herself, twiddling her thumbs and waiting for something exciting to happen.

She wasn't an old woman. At least, she didn't feel old, aside from the aching back and the knees that clicked when she stood up after sitting down for too long.

She knew that she needed to find something more to do with her life, because she couldn't spend the next thirty years sitting in that empty old house, waiting to die.

Both of her sons wanted her to move closer. They didn't want her to move in with them, but they wanted her to move closer. It was a nice thought, and she would have loved to have been around family, but moving would be a lot of work. It would take a lot of money that she didn't have. It would mean leaving the home that she had made for herself. It would mean moving to a place that had harsh winters. It would mean not knowing how to get anywhere or do anything.

Her boys made it sound so simple when they suggested that she move, but just the thought of it made her tired. She didn't know where she would begin such a move, so she just didn't do it at all.

She tried to distract herself by tending to her garden and making some small repairs around the house. As time passed, however, she began to feel isolated. The feeling was almost physical, as though her clothes were shrinking around her,

SHE DANCED

squeezing her, making it hard to breathe. It felt as though her house were growing smaller by the minute. It felt as if the rest of the world had ceased to exist when she wasn't paying attention.

Once she grew tired of feeling this way, Maureen walked out of her house and got into her car. She drove aimlessly, just looking from building to building, and store to store, waiting to feel a pull toward any of them.

When that didn't happen, she stopped for lunch.

Rather than go to a restaurant and sit by herself, Maureen decided to go to one of those big, members-only, warehouse stores.

She rarely shopped at places like this, since she didn't need to buy many things in bulk anymore, but she knew that they served pizza, and she knew that she could spend some time wandering through the store afterward, working off some calories.

Honestly, she didn't know why she stopped there. It just seemed different, and she needed to do something different. The old ways weren't working anymore.

Her lunch consisted of a slice of pizza and a churro—not the healthiest of meals, but good enough.

As she sat at one of the metal tables in the front of the store, eating her food, Maureen watched shoppers walk past with carts that were overflowing with frozen waffles and toilet paper.

She watched as each of those carts moved toward the exit, and she watched as a woman by the door examined shopper receipts, glanced at their carts, scribbled some sort of mark on the receipts, and then moved on.

As she watched this, she thought to herself that the woman's job looked so easy. She told herself that she could do a job like that, no problem.

And so, over the course of an hour, Maureen talked herself into approaching the customer service desk, and she asked for an application.

A week later, she was standing by that door, scribbling on receipts and telling people to have a nice day. She did this for four hours per day, five days per week.

She made conversation with coworkers. As time passed, she celebrated birthdays with some of the girls at the store. She was asked to put her name in a card for one of the girls who had recently given birth.

It wasn't much of a job. All she had to do was count the number of items in the cart and match it to the number on the receipt, but most of the people who did the job didn't even bother to count.

Her back hurt from standing for long stretches, but in some strange way, Maureen loved it. She loved that this was her life, which she had made for herself, even if it was small. Even if some of the people who walked through that store treated her as if she were nothing.

One day, as Maureen was walking into the store before her shift, she happened to glance toward the display of televisions that were being sold near the front door.

SHE DANCED

The biggest of those TVs was tuned into a cable channel, which was reporting on the death of 1950's teen icon Annie Wheeler.

Maureen's heart skipped a beat, and she stopped to watch the report on the screen.

As she watched, the reporter told viewers that Annie was perhaps best known for her musical romps of the later 50's and early 60's. She was America's sweetheart, often paired with Danny Finch. The two of them made six films together and dated for several years before splitting up for good in 1967.

The report went on, and a montage of Annie's work played on the screen. Watching Annie on screen, it wasn't hard to see why she was America's sweetheart. Her smile was infectious. Her laugh could be heard through any crowd.

A woman approached and stood by Maureen's side, also watching the report. This woman was about the same age as Maureen, but dressed in much nicer clothes. Her diamond ring was probably worth more than Maureen's car.

She was one of the people that had always treated Maureen poorly as she rushed to get out of the store and didn't want to be bothered with having her receipts checked.

Now, that woman was watching the screen as though she had suffered a great personal tragedy.

On the screen, one of Annie's earlier works appear. A children's variety show from the 1950's, filled with young performers who would put on a show every week for an audience of millions.

"I used to love that show," the woman said quietly, with a fond smile on her lips. "I dreamed of being one of those kids up there, singing and dancing…"

On the TV, Annie smiled and sang and danced, while a much younger Maureen swayed in the background.

∞

By 1957, Maureen had begun to feel like an old pro around whatever movie set she was on. Now she watched as younger kids came to work unsure of where to go or how to behave, and she always felt some responsibility to show them the ropes.

Other people told her that she should pay more attention to her own career, and stop helping other kids climb the ladder ahead of her.

Maureen ignored those people and told them that if it was that easy for someone to get ahead of her in this race, maybe they deserved it more than she did.

The smart move was to diversify her usefulness on set. Over the years, she'd met so many men and women who had come to Hollywood in the hopes of becoming a big star and failed to achieve that status, yet still managed to build a comfortable life for themselves in other departments.

SHE DANCED

Frank was one of those people, but he never would have dreamed of making the suggestion outright to Maureen. To do so would have gotten him into trouble with her mother, who was still holding out hope for the big house, with swimming pools and tennis courts.

It was a lot of pressure for Maureen, since all of her mother's dreams landed on her shoulders, but she was used to it by then. She was fourteen. Perhaps too old to be the new Shirley Temple, but just about the right age to be the next Liz Taylor.

Maureen was working steadily, and doing school work where she could, though she never got the formal education that she should have.

As she walked across the studio lot, on her way to walk across the background of some movie or another, she would wave to crew members along the way, and make small talk when she could. She knew some of the directors too. She had done more than her share of stand-in work, and even had more prominent background roles, playing the best friend of a lead role. She was one of the gang on set, though she still hadn't uttered a word on camera.

Other girls would have hated this. She'd seen so many of them get frustrated with the lack of forward momentum, and just vanish from the job entirely. Some left to pursue theater, thinking that it would be easier. Some left to become professional singers.

It seemed to Maureen that it was better for her to be on a film set, and to show people that she was reliable, than to walk away and show people that she was unwilling to do the thankless work.

This philosophy paid off one day, early in the year. Maureen was sitting in the holding area, where they kept all of the background actors for the day, just finishing up her lunch. She was by herself, singing a quiet little song absentmindedly, under her breath, when a man walking by stopped beside her.

She didn't notice him for several seconds, but when she did, she nearly jumped out of her skin.

After apologizing, the man sat down with her. His name was Arthur Crumb. He knew Maureen from several of the projects that she'd worked on, though she didn't know him very well. He'd been working his way up the ranks, doing different types of thankless jobs of his own. Now, he was a full-fledged producer.

Arthur told her that he'd just taken a job for one of the big networks, to create a variety show of sorts, with kids as their target audience. The show would feature a cast of young talent, who would perform different acts each week. Sometimes a comedy bit, sometimes a song or dance.

Maureen's heart began to pound in her chest. She'd heard about this sort of conversation, but she'd never actually been a part of one.

"I can't dance too well," Maureen told the man, worried about him finding out later.

SHE DANCED

He smiled and waved it off. He told her that he'd been going around the lot, asking different crew members that he knew if they had any suggestions for kids who might work on a show like that. Real hard workers, because it wasn't going to be an easy job for any of them.

Time and time again, her name came up.

As he told her that, Maureen became incredibly self-conscious. She'd always believed that she was blending into the background and not drawing attention to herself. She thought that was why people liked her at work. Now, she was discovering that all of those people saw something in her, and it nearly made her cry.

"Now, I'm not offering you a role outright," Arthur told her. "I'm offering you a chance to audition. We haven't put out a wide call for this one. We're hoping to grab some known talent before we open the madhouse doors. Do you think you're up for it?"

Maureen nodded and mumbled what she hoped was a good response, though she could hardly hear herself over the sound of her pounding heart. Her hands were sweating. Her mind was racing.

Arthur scribbled down a day and time for her audition, handed it to Maureen, and rushed off to find his next talent for the day.

That note remained in Maureen's pocket for the next ten hours, as she waited for work to be completed and for Frank to pick her up.

She sat quietly in his car as he drove the two of them home, and she waited patiently for her mother to arrive home an hour or two later.

As the family ate dinner together and her parents discussed their work, her mother turned to Maureen and asked her if anything exciting had happened on set that day.

Maureen had been waiting for that question all evening, and she'd planned exactly how she was going to tell her mother and Frank about her chat with Arthur.

When her mother asked the question, Maureen's heart began pounding again. She nodded and told her family, "A producer tracked me down at lunch today, because he wanted to request that I audition for one of the star roles in his new television series. It's a pretty exclusive audition too. That's all."

Her mother's eyes went wide, and she dropped her fork. She started asking Maureen so many questions that Maureen couldn't even keep up with all of them. When was the audition? What did she have to prepare? What would she wear? How would she do her hair?

While her mother was asking all of these questions, Frank was looking over the note that Arthur had given her, and he nodded to Maureen's mother.

"I've heard of this," he said to them. "This is the real deal. They pulled Chrissy Ford and Tim Lincoln aside to talk to them too."

SHE DANCED

Maureen knew those names well. They were day players—not quite as thankless a job as being an extra, but still low ranking. They were the kids who got to say a line or two, here and there.

Hearing this bit of news only served to make Maureen more nervous, and her mother more excited.

The two of them spent the next week preparing a cute song for Maureen to perform, and a nice dress for her to wear. Maureen was known as being reliable and well mannered at work, so they made her look like the sweet and adorable girl next door.

When the day came for her to go in there and audition, she was nervous, but there was also a strange sense of calm about this particular audition. When she walked into the office, she didn't see a whole room full of girls who looked exactly like her. She didn't have the same script that all of them would be reading.

Instead, she saw a room filled with a variety of kids, some of whom were already familiar to her. They all looked different, and they'd all prepared something different to show the producers.

In some way, it didn't feel like an audition to her—at least, not like the auditions that she'd been on before. She had been selected for this. They wanted her to succeed, because if she didn't, they would have to audition hundreds of other kids, while she just went back to work as usual.

The audition was almost fun. The producers called her in, and Arthur asked her a few questions about herself. She told them who she was, and where she had come from, and how grateful she was for the opportunity to perform for them.

She spoke with purpose and sincerity, which had always been her downfall in an industry that thrived on big personalities and self-promotion, but the adults in the room responded well to her. One woman even called her cute.

When she performed her song for them, she held her hands behind her back and swayed a little bit, but didn't dare dance.

Arthur asked her why she didn't like to dance, and she shyly told him that she was known for tripping over her own two feet when she tried. She told him that she'd once spun herself right into a wall, which made everyone in the room chuckle.

Then they thanked her for her time, and they sent her on her way.

Maureen wasn't sure whether or not this was a good audition for her. It certainly wasn't what she was used to. And she didn't hold her breath, waiting to hear whether or not she got the job. She simply went back to her normal routine, with her normal work.

Days passed, and she began to hear whispers about the other kids who had auditioned. One of them supposedly broke down in tears when the producers tried making normal conversation with him. He hadn't prepared for that part, and nobody had ever taught him how to be a regular person.

She was walking across the lot, on her way home one day, when she saw Arthur coming in the other direction. She smiled politely and waved at him as he walked by, and he did the same.

SHE DANCED

Then he stopped and said, "Oh, Maureen… I almost forgot to tell you…"

She stopped and turned around to face him.

He smiled and told her, "We'd love to have you on our show, if you're available."

For a moment, she was caught off balance and asked, "You mean, in the background?"

Arthur laughed and said, "I mean under the spotlight."

Then, after assuring her that he would be in touch with her people, he said goodbye and left Maureen by herself.

She stood in stunned silence for several minutes, replaying the conversation in her head and trying to figure out whether he had actually said what she thought he'd said, or if she had somehow misunderstood.

When the daze began to lift and Maureen realized what had just happened, she took a few deep breaths and looked around the lot, seeing dozens of people going about their work, so she didn't want to scream.

Instead, she started walking across the lot. She walked faster and faster by the second, until she was running.

She ran to the parking lot, where her mother was standing by their car, waiting for her, and she jumped into her mother's arms and sobbed.

"Maureen?" her mother asked, not knowing why her daughter was crying, or why she was clinging to her. "What happened? Did someone hurt you? Did they—"

"I got the part!" Maureen cut in, and then pulled back to look her mother in the eyes. "I got the part."

Her mother's eyes went wide, and the woman did all of the screaming that Maureen had been too afraid to do herself.

They jumped up and down and hugged each other, and then they both stopped to lean against the car. Both of them took deep breaths.

It had been a decade since they left home. They'd worked themselves nearly to death. They'd sacrificed so much in order to pursue this crazy, absurd dream.

Now, here it was. The work wasn't over, but the question of whether or not it was even possible had finally been answered. Their sacrifices were justified.

This was it. This moment was what success felt like. It wouldn't last. Reality would have to settle in at some point. But for just that moment, they were living the dream.

∞

Maureen stood in the foyer of her home, staring at the front door, not sure what to do next.

It was October, 1998. She'd just watched her second child, Sean, drive off to another state, and another life. Somewhere far away from Maureen and her husband, Bill, and despite everyone promising to see each other often, and to call every week, she knew that life would get in the way. It always did.

SHE DANCED

She'd been through this once before already. She'd even done it to her own mother, back in the day. It was hard back then, but to be on the other side of it was a different type of pain altogether. It was as though someone had taken a vital organ out of her body, and now she had to learn how to live without that organ.

She didn't know how to be something other than a mother. Even when her kids had their own apartments and houses, she'd still been there. She'd still babysat her granddaughter. She'd still cooked family meals and brought groceries over to their houses. She still took care of her family, because that was who she was.

How was she supposed to be that person now?

When she turned away from the front door, Bill was standing right behind her, watching her as though she were about to break in two. Behind him, there were coat hooks on the wall, where she had hung her sons' coats since they were small children. She could almost see those coats still hanging there. The bright red and blue one that made little Sean feel like Superman. The brown and green one that reminded Ian of army men. The black wool peacoat that Ian always wore in college. The leather biker jacket that Sean was wearing just a few days earlier.

Bill took a step toward Maureen and put his hands on her hips as he looked her in the eyes. He didn't say anything to her, because he didn't have to. Somehow, he had always been capable of speaking volumes to Maureen without opening his mouth, and now she could see that he was just as lost as she was.

She put her head on his chest, and he held her close for a while. When she closed her eyes, she focused on the sound of his breathing. The rise and fall. The beating of his heart.

He was still there, and he wasn't going anywhere. She wasn't alone. She still had a purpose and a reason.

When she opened her eyes, the first thing she saw were the scratches on the hardwood floor, where their dog, Harvey, had tried to dig his way to a mouse twenty years earlier.

It was so strange to Maureen, to be on this side of her life, looking back. She'd pictured a day like this for as long as she'd had children, but it always seemed like a far-off idea. It was always the thing that she didn't want to talk about or think about, because it had always been something that she didn't have to worry about yet.

Now it was here. She was in the moment, and it wasn't what she expected. It wasn't sobbing and sharp pain. It was just quiet, and empty.

Each time she blinked her eyes, she could see the past thirty years flash before her eyes, as if they were the lightning in a storm that was raging within her own mind.

Just a moment ago, she was a young mother, stepping through that door for the first time, while looking at one more house that she and her husband might purchase.

Now, she was an old woman, with kids and a grandkid who lived far away.

SHE DANCED

Bill put his hands on either side of Maureen's face, and looked into her eyes.

"How's it going in there?" he asked her, breaking the silence that she'd been living in for what felt like years.

She didn't say anything in response. She just nodded, to let him know that she would be all right, and she tried to smile, but she couldn't quite pull it off.

When he looked at her that way, she could still see the young man that he had been when she first met him. He was a police officer back then, tall and muscular. She'd always thought that he would become a detective and chase down bad guys, like they did in the movies. She didn't like the idea of it, but she loved him enough to put up with the worry.

Then he was in a car accident, and he wasn't a cop anymore. He went to work in an office, doing a job that she never quite understood, and before she knew it, they had this house, which sat on acres of land that all belonged to them.

She worried about him in a different way after that. She always kept an eye on him, wondering if he was miserable with this new life, but he never showed any sign of it.

"Let's go for a walk," he said to her. Then he smiled and added, "The house is too loud."

He took her by the hand and the two of them walked out the same door that their son had just gone through. They walked down the porch steps and into the yard.

The sun was shining bright. It was cool, but not cold. The perfect day for a picnic with the boys, if only it were possible.

She and Bill walked slowly, across the property that had now been theirs for longer than any of their neighbors had lived nearby.

The land was just as full of memories as the house. As they walked, they passed by the remains of a chicken coop, which had long ago collapsed and was now being swallowed by tall grass and weeds.

They passed the clearing where a swing set once stood. The swing set had been gone for ten years. Now there were bales of hay and archery targets that had been torn to shreds.

When Maureen looked toward the old shed, where they kept their lawn tools, she could almost see another dog, Bernie, barking at a rattlesnake.

"We should get a dog," she said to Bill as they continued to walk. "We haven't had a dog in a long time."

Bill smiled and said, "We could get some chickens again too. And a goat."

"No goat!" Maureen shot back.

They'd had a goat once, and it had proven to be far more trouble than it was worth.

Bill laughed at the memory of the old goat, and took Maureen's hand.

"You did good," he told her.

"I did what good?" she asked.

SHE DANCED

"All of it. The whole damn thing. I have spent the past thirty-five years in awe of you."

She started to laugh, as though he were telling the funniest joke in the world. From her perspective, she had been stumbling through motherhood and marriage, with absolutely no idea what she was doing, and more often than not, she was certain that she was making all of the wrong decisions.

Bill was the one who kept them going. When he lost one job, he got another, and he worked hard to give them everything they could want.

They walked down to a little creek that ran through their property, and sat on a small bench that they'd set up years earlier, so they could watch the boys play in the water.

Bill took a deep breath and looked up at the sky. As he did this, he pulled Maureen's hand up to his mouth and kissed it.

She wrapped her arm around his and pulled herself closer to him.

"We could move," he told her. "Closer to them, I mean."

"Which one? They live in different states," she replied.

"Maybe somewhere in the middle?"

"Still hours away."

"We could get a motorhome, and bounce back and forth."

Maureen laughed at that.

"We could start a business together, to occupy our time," she told him.

"Yeah? What would we do?"

Maureen took a deep breath, and thought about the possibilities. Then she said, "Private detectives."

Bill didn't laugh. He considered the possibility for a few seconds, before nodding and saying, "I guess I could clear out some space in the barn, for an office. We don't want clients like that coming into the house."

"Oh, I hadn't thought of that."

"You have to think about those details when you're a PI."

"I'll learn."

"I was thinking that we might start smaller. Get some honey bees. Sell honey down at the farmer's market," Bill said.

"Doesn't sound as fun as solving murders."

Bill shook his head and told her, "Most of the detective work is cheating spouses. We'd spend all night taking pictures of strangers having sex."

Maureen cringed at the thought, and said, "I do like honey."

"Who doesn't like honey?" Bill asked. "We can put honey in coffee and tea. Use it to make honey cake, and honey ice cream. Honey pie…"

"Honey buns," she added.

Bill nodded, as though he were adding honey buns to the list of menu items in his mind.

They went on, talking about the plans for their honey farm, for the next couple of hours. They talked about clearing all of the tall grass off of the property and planting wildflowers, so their bees could have more pollen. They spoke about planting fruit trees, because the bees would be good for growing fruit, and then they could add fresh fruit to all of their honey-themed baked goods.

They talked about how nice it would be to have some milking cows, but not right away. Maybe in a few years, once they had a handle on the bees and the fruit trees.

Then they spent some time trying to think up a name for their new business. Danvers Farm seemed too obvious, so they wanted to find something more clever.

"Happy Fun Time Farm?" Bill suggested.

Maureen punched him in the arm.

For that afternoon, as they sat there, the future was full of possibilities. They were planning and dreaming, the same way they had when they were first married. In their joint imagination, they built up a whole new business for themselves, which would lead them into the next phase of their life together.

It was a beautiful dream.

There wouldn't be a farm, of course. No honey bees, no farmer's market empire.

What they were doing was distracting themselves from the reality of what their lives were now. How many people built entirely new lives for themselves after age fifty? How many people learned new skills?

Maureen didn't know what the future looked like. She'd only planned as far as raising her kids and seeing them off. She never thought about much after that. She didn't know how to be a grandmother from across the country. She didn't know how to be a mother by telephone.

"We should plant some flowers out front," she said to Bill, as they walked back toward the house that day.

Bill took a deep breath and said, "That sounds like a lot of work. Can we do it tomorrow?"

She smiled again, and asked him, "Do you think we're old?"

"I think we were old ten years ago," Bill replied.

She accepted that answer, because it was pretty fair. They didn't go out to clubs, or host big parties for their friends and neighbors anymore. They had settled into a routine of watching Wheel of Fortune with dinner, and falling asleep to Leno, and Maureen didn't expect that to change very much in the near future.

One might have expected her to be saddened by that fact. They might think that she would be sad to realize that those big dreams for the future were nothing more than a fantasy, shared between an old married couple.

She wasn't sad though.

What she realized that day was that her life wasn't over, and it hadn't collapsed around her when her sons moved away.

When they walked into the house that afternoon, she remembered being carried over the threshold when they first moved in. She remembered all the nights where children were crying because of nightmares, or vomiting because of some bug that they'd caught at school.

SHE DANCED

She remembered making coffee early in the morning, while Bill showered and got ready for work.

She remembered being a young woman, and dreaming of the life that she would share with that man.

As sad as she was to see her kids move away, Maureen took comfort in knowing that Bill was still by her side. They would figure out this new life together, just as they had figured out all the rest of it.

At times, the memories contained within the walls of that house would make her heart ache, but she wouldn't trade that ache for anything in the world.

This was her life. It was quiet and simple, and she loved it.

∞

There were times when something so big and important happened, that Maureen believed that her life was going to change forever. She would look at those moments from a distance, and couldn't imagine how she could ever arrive at such a point without becoming something entirely new.

Usually, she would come to realize that no matter how far she had come, she would always be the same person. Reliable, sure. Talented even. Yet, she was always that girl who sat in the corner and watched as everyone else played the game so much better than she ever could.

Then there were moments which seemed insignificant at first glance, but wound up transforming her world.

The Happy Slappy Fun Time Kids Variety Hour—shortened to The Happy Fun Time Show several years later—was an example of something that should have changed how she saw herself, but it didn't.

She was fifteen now, and had been working on the show for nearly a year. She and the rest of the cast would arrive on Monday morning, receive their assignments for the week, and then head off for rehearsals for a few days. On Thursday, they would have a dress rehearsal, wherein they would perform the entire show for the week, and film anything that needed to be pre-prepared, and then they would perform the show live on Saturday evening.

The show was broadcast across the entire country, which meant that Maureen's family back home could see the young woman that she had become.

Her mother would have them tune in every week, and quiz them on the phone afterwards, just to prove that they were paying attention to the star of the family.

Maureen didn't like having people talking about her so much. It made her feel self-conscious, and that was the last thing she needed.

She was famous, in a way. She'd been recognized by a little girl at the drug store once, and the show was popular enough to keep going.

SHE DANCED

At first, it was hard to tell just how popular the show was, because she and the other kids were always working. They only had one real day off per week, and most of their down time in between rehearsals and performances was spent on the studio lot, with each other. It was hard to see how the world was responding to their show, if it was responding at all.

And so, working on the show was just like working on any other project for Maureen. She would show up, sit around for most of her day, and then perform when she was told to perform. The only difference now was that she got to speak on camera.

It was nice. She knew most of the crew, and felt comfortable working on the show. She worried that she wouldn't be prepared for whatever job they handed her next, but when the time came, she was always up to the challenge.

The producers knew each of the kids well, and knew what they were capable of. Some were better dancers than singers. Some were better at performing comedy sketches. Some were the regular singers on the show.

A few of the kids could do a little of each, and a couple of them were the standout performers. The ones who could do whatever was asked of them.

Annie Wheeler was one of the standouts. She could sing, dance and act just as well as anyone on the show. Being one of the older kids, Annie was usually paired with Ollie Maxwell for the big song and dance numbers. Ollie wasn't quite as talented a singer as

Annie, but she made him look better than he was, and the pair was everyone's favorite to watch.

Annie was also beautiful, and the studio loved her because as she got older, they saw the chance to use her in other television shows and movies. She was almost seventeen by the time the first season of the show was wrapped and the kids went on their one-month break.

Rumor had it that Annie might get her own sitcom before the show came back, but the deal fell through and Annie stayed put.

It was just as well. Maureen loved watching Annie work. She admired not just the talent, but the desire to push harder and do more. It was something that Maureen never felt within herself.

That first break in between seasons was the first time that Maureen had the chance to watch the show on television, just like everyone else. The network was playing reruns, and Maureen happened to be home one Saturday when it was on.

Her parents were out of the house, so Maureen watched alone. It was a surreal experience, to see people that she knew well on TV. To see how the numbers were edited together, and the overall energy of the show. She smiled as she watched, because it was designed to make people smile. It was sweet, and charming, and fun.

Maureen felt proud of the show as she sat there. She loved that she got to be a part of something that she herself could enjoy.

And then she saw herself on screen.

SHE DANCED

It wasn't that she looked bad, or that her performance was awful. The thing that pulled Maureen out of her excitement for the show was the fact that she was just standing there, under a spotlight, singing her little song while swaying back and forth like an idiot.

Annie had been tossed into the air by Ollie and still managed to sing, while Maureen couldn't even manage one spin during her performance.

Doubt was something that had never bothered Maureen before. She did the job that she was given, and then she moved on with her life. But now, she was watching some real talent on screen, and she felt like the weak link in the chain.

As the show went on, Maureen saw herself pop up in one of the comedy sketches, and she managed a chuckle. She wasn't mortified by her line reading, which was some consolation.

However, when she went to bed that night, Maureen thought about the image of herself standing on that stage, under that spotlight, and it made her cringe.

As her break continued, Maureen avoided watching the show, but she couldn't avoid hearing about it. Just sitting in a diner with her mother one day, the two of them overheard two young girls talking about the show. Maureen's mother smiled from ear to ear, and looked as though she were about to go and force an autograph on those other girls, but that didn't happen.

Maureen smiled too, but in a different way. To see her mother light up like that, with such excitement and such pride, made Maureen feel as if she had finally been able to give her mother the thing that she had wanted for as long as Maureen had been alive.

After all of the struggle, and all of the doubt, here they were. It was wonderful.

The break came to an end far too quickly. While the show wouldn't premiere for another few weeks, the producers wanted to bring the kids in and get a head start on pre-filming some sketches and rehearsing some new numbers.

They also wanted to introduce the existing cast members to a couple of new kids who would be joining the team. Over the break, two of the kids had taken other jobs, so they wouldn't be back. In their place were Bittie Swan and Mike Hanley.

Bittie was perhaps a year or two younger than Maureen, with freckles and bright red hair. Maureen imagined that Bittie's mother had insisted that the girl might be the next Shirley Temple, and the thought made her smile.

Mike was just about Maureen's age, with neatly combed blond hair, and blue eyes. The all-American boy next door.

Both of the new additions proved their worth. Maureen and Mike were paired up for a comedy routine, which was pretty straight-forward and easy to learn.

In the sketch, Maureen would be playing the waitress in a diner, while Mike played a boy who had been out in the wilderness for a week without food or water. She would bring him a drink, but each time he attempted to take it from her, she would get distracted and turn away, leaving him to suffer for just a little bit longer.

They ran through the scene with one of their producers that day, taking notes on how each of them should behave, and how the tension should build within the scene. Maureen was instructed to play stupid, as if she couldn't tell that the boy was on the verge of death.

She did as they were told, and the two of them shared a few laughs as they went through their rehearsal. This would be one of the pre-filmed sketches for the week, which would give everyone more time to prepare for the live segments.

Her first impression of the new kid was that he was talented, and he sure seemed to know it too. It wasn't that he was rude, or anything like that, but Maureen got the impression that Mike had been told how great he was from a very early age.

Apparently, the feeling was mutual.

During their lunch break, as Maureen was sitting by herself and eating a sandwich that she had brought from home, Annie approached and sat down beside her.

Annie had a conspiratorial look on her face, as though she didn't want anyone else to know what the two girls were talking about.

"The new boy thinks you're a bit of a snob," Annie told her, with a sly grin.

"What? Me?" Maureen replied, genuinely shocked.

She didn't like the idea of people talking about her behind her back, so learning that people were saying unkind things was especially frustrating.

"Well," Annie said. "Not a snob, really. He just think that you believe you're better than us. Sitting alone, watching everyone work, as though you're sizing us up."

Annie laughed as she said this, because she knew how absurd the notion was.

"Oh, don't worry. I told him that you're just the quiet type. I told him that you're the nicest girl I know."

Maureen smiled at that part. Annie pulled an apple out of her pocket and started to eat with Maureen. They made pleasant conversation about what they'd done over the break, with Annie going on and on about scripts and managers.

Annie loved the work, but hated the business side of things. She wanted to leave that up to the adults, but they sure did make it hard sometimes.

When she asked Maureen what she'd been doing while they were away, Maureen told her about all of the simple things. Reading books and walking through the park. Going to the beach, and watching television.

She told Annie that she saw the show, and was amazed at how much she enjoyed watching it.

Annie laughed and said that she could never watch herself. She would drive herself crazy, looking for all of the little things that she'd done wrong.

SHE DANCED

Maureen forced a smile at this part. She didn't want to talk about the reaction she'd had to seeing herself. She was embarrassed by what she'd seen, and wished that it would go away. Part of her didn't even feel like she belonged on the show anymore, but she didn't say any of that to Annie.

"We're going out later tonight," Annie told Maureen. "A few of us older kids are going to some old camping spot to roast hot dogs and goof off. You should come."

Maureen was caught off guard by this. She had never been invited out with the older kids before. She'd always thought of herself as being one of the younger kids, just watching the others from a distance. She wasn't sure why she felt that way, since she wasn't especially young. She just never felt like she belonged with the more experienced performers.

"Oh, I don't know. I'd have to see if I'm allowed," Maureen replied, trying to think up a good excuse to get out of going.

"Well, I hope you can. We're not doing anything too crazy. We just want to have some fun before the hard work begins."

"I'll try," Maureen said.

Then Annie had to go. She was rehearsing yet another big number with Ollie. It would consume most of her week, learning all of those spins and leaps.

Meanwhile, Maureen was pretty sure that she had her comedy bit down already. Clearly, one of these girls was putting in more work than the other.

She wasn't even sure why it was bothering her. She could sing and act just as well as anyone, and nobody had ever made her feel bad about her inability to dance. The only thing that had changed was the fact that she now felt as if she wasn't pulling her weight on that show. If she couldn't do that, maybe she didn't belong there in the first place.

At the end of the day, Maureen was hoping to slip out unnoticed, and get home for a quiet dinner with her family. She'd almost done it too, but as she made her way toward the parking lot, she heard someone call her name behind her.

When she turned around, she saw Mike rushing to catch up.

"On your way out?" he asked.

Maureen nodded.

"Me too," he said, a bit awkwardly. Then he said, "I just wanted to let you know how glad I am to be working with you. I was worried that they'd put me with the kids when I first got here."

"If there's anything I can do to help you settle in, let me know," Maureen offered.

"Thanks. You know, I've seen the show. You're pretty good on it."

Maureen looked away, once again seeing herself standing under that spotlight, singing. She tried not to appear as though the thought bothered her. She just smiled and thanked him.

Then Mike looked down at the ground and asked, "Are you going out with the other kids tonight? A couple of them asked me if I wanted to go to some park or something."

SHE DANCED

Maureen smiled, "I don't think so. I'm pretty busy at home, and I want to get some rest before we have to work tomorrow."

Mike chuckled at that, as if he knew how easy their job was, compared to all of the other kids who were putting on big song and dance numbers.

He caught himself in that chuckle, and quickly stopped. He said, "I didn't mean to laugh. I'm grateful to be here."

She wasn't sure what to make of that comment, or the boy who had made it. Part of her felt as though he were thinking the same thing that she was. As though they were in on the same joke together.

But some other part of her wondered if he believed himself to be too good for the job they'd been given. As though working at her level were beneath him.

Maureen straightened up, and told Mike, "It seems easy now, but it's going to get hard very quickly. In a month or two, you will be begging for a break."

Mike nodded and again said, "I didn't mean to sound ungrateful. It's taken me a long time to get here, and I don't plan on throwing it away."

"Good," Maureen said. "Now, I'm going to go and rest."

She started to walk away, but Mike hurried to keep up with her and walked by her side.

"You can call me Mick, by the way," he told her. "It's my real name."

Maureen was puzzled. She asked, "If that's your real name, why aren't you using it for the show?"

"Because the producers thought it would remind people of some other show, with some other—"

"Oh," Maureen cut in, finally understanding. She smiled and said, "So you have to use a whole new name?"

"Sorta. I mean, my full name is Michael."

Maureen nodded again. She asked him, "How do you spell that?"

Mick shrugged and started to respond, "M-I-C…"

He then caught himself and stopped, which made Maureen laugh.

She put up a hand and said, "I'm sorry. I didn't mean to be rude."

He didn't reply right away. They just kept walking together, which Maureen found strange. She was going to meet Frank, which meant that Mick certainly wasn't headed in the same direction, yet he kept walking by her side.

"Be honest," he finally said, breaking the silence between them. "Are the other kids okay? I mean, are they just luring me out tonight so that they can pull some prank, or make the new kid look stupid?"

"We've all met those kids," Maureen sighed. "But no. I haven't seen anyone act that way in our group. The younger kids can be a little bratty when they're tired, but that's all."

"I can be bratty when I'm tired too."

SHE DANCED

"I bet."

"So, will you come out with us?"

Maureen stopped walking and asked, "Why is it so important that I go with you?"

Mick grinned and said, "You're the only one I've been talking to since I got here. Besides, it'll be fun. If they don't hang me upside down from a tree, I mean."

After thinking about it for a moment, Maureen agreed to go. After all, it wasn't every day that she got invited to go along with the other kids, and she didn't want to seem like a snob.

And so, Maureen let Frank know where she was going, and she and Mick waited for the other kids—including a boy named Randy and a girl named Violet—to finish up with their work for the day.

Once everyone was finished, they loaded into Ollie's car—three up front and three in the back—and they headed off for their night of fun.

They wound up at an old campsite, outside of the city. They were surrounded by trees, and no other people. They weren't the most famous celebrities in town, but if they were seen together at the beach, they would have attracted more attention than they wanted, and they would have been forced to put on a show for the crowd. According to Annie, that was what happened the last time the older kids went out together, and it ruined their night.

As it was, the evening was warm and quiet. They started a little campfire, and gathered around it. They roasted hot dogs on sticks, which surprised Maureen. She'd just assumed that Annie was making that part up.

There was beer being passed around, but neither Maureen nor Mick drank any of it. If her mother smelled beer on her breath when she got home, she would be in a world of trouble.

As for Mick… He just shrugged and said that he didn't like the stuff.

Ollie brought a guitar with him, and so the whole gang spent hours singing silly songs, and imagining Arthur's reaction if any of them suggested putting a rock and roll song in the show.

Randy borrowed the guitar and performed his best version of *Jailhouse Rock*, while Annie and Violet pretended to swoon.

Maureen, Annie and Violet sang *Mr. Sandman*, and then Maureen sang *Tammy* by herself.

As she sang it, she looked into the fire, and the memory of seeing herself under that spotlight came back to her. It made her feel self-conscious, but she tried her best not to show it.

Mick sang *Love, Love, Love* while Randy played the guitar. Annie and Violet giggled and danced together as he sang it, which made everyone laugh.

It was a good night. It was nothing like what Maureen imagined it would be. Somehow, she pictured more alcohol and the other kids slobbering all over each other. Oh, Randy and Violet did wander off eventually, and Annie and Ollie retreated to their own little world, but that didn't happen until later in the night.

SHE DANCED

Once the singing and laughing had died down a bit, Maureen wandered away from the group, lost in her own thoughts.

She didn't remember the last time she'd been away from big buildings and the sounds of cars speeding by. The woods were peaceful and calm. The sky was full of stars. It reminded her of a home that she didn't even remember.

"Can I ask you a question," Mick asked as he approached, startling Maureen back to reality.

"I suppose so," she replied.

"Well, like I said before, I've seen the show. I know how talented everyone is, and… Well, I was just wondering why you never dance. Even tonight, you didn't dance with the others."

"I don't like dancing."

"Who doesn't like dancing?"

"A girl who's been known to fall on her face, and spin into posts, that's who."

"You're telling me that you can't dance? Not at all?"

"Mm-hmm."

"I don't believe that."

"Well, you should. My mother put me in classes when I was four years old. At five years old, my teacher declared me unteachable," Maureen explained. She then put on a thick accent and said, "Your feet are like little blocks of cement, stuck to the ends of two broomsticks, tied to the body of a dead cow."

Mick smiled from ear to ear and said, "Mrs. Thorp. I know her. Real witch, if you ask me."

"Well, I believed her. And all of the other kids believed her, and so I just…"

Maureen trailed off. Mick cocked his head just slightly and asked, "You what?"

She shrugged in response and said, "I didn't want to dance anyway. I was tired. Eventually, my mother even gave up on me."

Mick nodded as though he suddenly understood some big secret, and he said, "You stopped dancing out of revenge."

"I did not."

"You did so. Your mother had you in classes when you were that young. That tells me that you never asked for it. I wouldn't be surprised if you didn't even want to be on the show."

Maureen took a step toward Mick and glared at him as she said, "How dare you? You don't know me at all."

Mick shrugged and said, "I didn't mean anything by it. I'm not sure that any of us chose to be here."

"Don't you want it?"

"Sure I do. But sometimes I wonder what it would be like to go to school, you know? Like a real kid."

"We are real kids."

Mick laughed at that.

They stopped talking for some time after that, both just looking at the world around them, and the stars overhead. Both trying to avoid looking back at the other kids, because they didn't want to know what they were up to.

SHE DANCED

Eventually, Mick broke the silence and said, "When I was a kid, my mother used to drive me past this old baseball field near where we lived. I'd always see other kids my age, diving in the dirt and hitting the ball, and I used to wonder what it was like. To just be a kid, playing with friends because you felt like it. Having fun, you know?"

"I used to watch the girls play hopscotch on the sidewalk outside of our apartment," Maureen replied.

"Ever play?" Mick asked her.

Maureen shrugged and said, "No. I was always being rushed off to my next class, or my next big audition."

Mick nodded. He then took a deep breath, and waved his hand through the air, declaring, "We are playing hopscotch."

"What?" Maureen asked. "We don't have chalk, or a sidewalk."

"We have our imaginations."

"Do you know how to play hopscotch?"

"No idea. Do you know how to play baseball?"

Maureen laughed and said, "No."

"Then we'll make it up."

Mick looked around and found a small stone, which he tossed onto the ground. He then hopped over to it, first on one foot, then on two, as though there were actually a hopscotch grid beneath his feet.

Maureen laughed at the absurdity of it.

"Your turn," Mick said.

She hesitated, but then nodded and looked around for a stone of her own. She tossed it, and then hopped through the imaginary grid.

"Well done," Mick declared. "Now we do the hard part."

"What hard part?"

"The backward hopscotch. It's how you win the game."

"I've never seen anyone do a backward hopscotch before."

Mick tossed a stone over his shoulder, and then hopped backward through his imaginary grid. Once he was done, he sighed a breath of relief.

Maureen wasn't going to let him win this game, so she did the same, nearly hitting him with her stone as she did it.

They played around like this for a few minutes, hopping back and forth, and looking like complete fools.

Then, Mick held out his hand and said, "Now we do the extremely difficult, forward-backward double hopscotch, to win the game."

Maureen took his hand and nodded as though this were a serious event. They were on the verge of winning the Olympic gold medal of hopscotch, and it all depended on this moment.

They hopped together, first with one foot, and then two, through the big, imaginary hopscotch grid, and then hopped backwards through it once again.

When they had completed their round of dual hopscotch, Mick tugged Maureen and spun her into his arms with great flourish.

SHE DANCED

He smiled at her, and said, "See? You can dance."

While she wanted to protest and once again inform him that she did not dance, Maureen had to stop herself, and admit that she did just dance with Mick, in a strange sort of way.

It was a silly, absurd dance, sure. It was not choreographed at all, and would never be presentable in front of an audience, but it was a dance, and she had enjoyed it. She had never enjoyed dancing before. It was an odd feeling.

A couple of days went by, and the two of them continued to work on their comedy routine together. She was the dopey waitress, and he was the starving man.

After some time, even that silly sketch started to feel more fun to Maureen. She and Mick would push the limits of their script, and the whole thing turned into a game of keep-away between them.

She almost felt bad about the way they were behaving. They were playing games, when they were supposed to be working, but the producers didn't mind. In fact, they were laughing more now than they had been at the start.

At lunch, she would sit by herself, but Mick was always somewhere nearby, deep in his own thoughts, just like her. Every so often, she would catch him looking at her with a sort of determined scowl, but then he would turn away when he noticed her looking his way.

She didn't know what that expression meant. It worried her a little bit, since he was clearly working up some scheme that involved her, but she said nothing about it.

Then, one day after work, as the two of them were walking toward the parking lot, Mick said to her, "You did dance, you know?"

"I was playing around, that's all," she replied.

"Isn't that what dancing is? Once you strip away the showy parts, I mean? All of those kids who go to school dances are just playing around, right?"

"They're not being judged for it."

This led to an argument about all of the things that would go wrong if she were to try doing this in front of people, but Mick just brushed aside all of Maureen's excuses.

"The whole comedy sketch that we're doing is a dance," he told her.

"It is not."

"What else do you call it when we're spinning and sliding and jumping all around each other like that?"

"I'd call it… stage direction."

"Well, I'd call it choreography. And we're pretty good at it too."

"Have you seen the dancers on the show? The way they float and glide…"

"We could do that."

SHE DANCED

"We?" Maureen asked. "Nobody ever said that you couldn't dance."

"Well, we're a team now. If you don't dance, I don't dance."

"Since when are we a team?"

"I don't know… Annie and Ollie get to be partners. Why can't we?"

Maureen didn't respond right away. The truth was, she'd never thought of having a partner before. She just showed up for work, and did whatever job they handed her. She was just fine, blending into the background.

Except, that was what she'd always done, and all it ever got her was that moment when she saw herself on TV, and felt stupid for even pretending to be on the same level as all of the others.

She also had to admit that working with Mick had been more fun than she'd ever had at work before.

"I really can't dance, Mick. I'm sorry, but I just can't," she told him.

"You know what I think?" Mick asked her. "I think that you never had a chance to enjoy any of this before."

"You don't know me."

"But I also think that you did enjoy it the other night, and what's so bad about that?"

"Nothing. I just can't dance, that's all."

"Then I'll teach you. Unless you're afraid or something."

"I am not afraid."

"Fine then, I'll teach you."

"Fine."

"And you'll have fun too!"

"Fine!"

"Fine!"

That moment would change the course of Maureen's life in more ways than she would ever realize. The way Mick could bring her out of her shell. The way he encouraged her to be better, but not in the same way that she'd been pushed before.

She did enjoy sitting around that fire, singing songs with friends. She did enjoy goofing around with Mick, and the strange dance that had come from their game of imaginary hopscotch.

It was the beginning of something big for her, and over the next couple of weeks, she and Mick worked together during their off hours, turning their game into something more.

The thing was, she knew the steps. She knew the concepts behind all of the different moves, because she had been in those classes, and had worked around dancers for years. Her mother had bought her books on dancing, even after she stopped going to the classes.

In her mind, Maureen knew how to dance. The trouble was getting her mind to work with her feet.

In the past, she was so worried about letting people down that she never allowed herself to enjoy dancing. It wasn't a game. It wasn't meant to be fun. It was the place where she was yelled at for doing something wrong. It was the place where she was made to feel stupid for not being as good as everyone else.

SHE DANCED

She had given herself over to being a bad dancer, because it meant that she wouldn't have to endure that torture anymore. It was the one thing that her mother had allowed her to fail at, and in some strange way, that failure had always felt like a win to Maureen. It was hers. It was the only part of this that she had chosen.

Which was fine, right up until it wasn't. Now she wanted to be better, because she didn't want to be just the girl who stood there under the spotlight anymore. She didn't want her movements to be nothing more than swaying back and forth behind the better performers.

As they worked together, Mick made her want to be the best, but he did it in a way that was fun. He allowed her to not just follow other peoples' ideas of what she should be doing, but to be herself. He allowed her personality to come through, and for the first time in her life, she felt as though *she* were being seen in the performance that she was giving.

He created a whole routine for them, based on the lives that they'd dreamed of having as kids. Playing ball, and hopscotch, and jumping rope, and running through a sunny field. He worked all of that into the dance, with spins and jumps, and he even added some comedy.

It was fun. Even when Maureen fell down—which she did quite often—she did so laughing, and the more time that they spent together, the more it felt as though she'd discovered that fun childhood that she'd never had before.

After a few weeks, she came to realize something else about Mick. He was her best friend. She'd never had a best friend before.

At work, the writers picked up on the chemistry that the two of them had in their performances, and they were paired in more and more skits together. Never dance numbers though, because it was still too soon for them to show the producers what they'd been working on.

She grew more comfortable moving like a dancer as time passed. When she was home alone, she would move the furniture out of the way, and she would practice the number that Mick had created for them. She would fall on her face every time she attempted a spin or dip without him there to catch her, but she always pulled herself back up, and she tried it again.

Once both she and Mick believed that they were ready, they pulled Arthur aside one day at lunch, and they showed him their dance.

Maureen was so nervous that morning, she nearly made herself sick, but when she was in front of Arthur, with her partner by her side, all of those nerves went away.

When she moved, she glided. When she spun and dipped, Mick was there to catch her. When they did the bit of hopscotch, Arthur laughed.

When it was over, they waited.

It didn't happen right away, but after a couple of weeks, they were handed a new act to work on together. They would

SHE DANCED

perform the dance that Mick had created, while singing a song that the show's writers had written to go along with it.

It felt as if fate itself had brought Maureen to this moment, with her best friend beside her.

Mike and Maureen debuted as an official partnership with that dance. From that point on, every comedy sketch they did, they did together. Every song was sung together. Every dance was performed together. Even when they were working with the rest of the kids, they were working together.

∞

It had been a long and strange journey, to get to this point in her life. She had walked away from everything she ever knew. She had married a police officer, and watched his world be turned upside down after being injured on the job.

She had watched him start all over again, with a new job and a new mission in life.

They were parents now. In the autumn of 1978, Sean was eleven years old, and Ian was nine. They had been living in an old farmhouse for a year by this point, still repairing and painting, and planning. There was so much planning to do in those days, because it felt as though the world had opened up in front of Maureen. Nothing was impossible.

As she pulled her hair into a ponytail, she looked at the roots in her mirror, and saw the light blonde beginning to show through. It had been dyed a dark chestnut brown for years—at first in rebellion, but then because it felt more like the person she had become.

It was Saturday. The first day in weeks when she would have a moment to catch her breath. Over the past month, she had been volunteering at her kids' school, working on the fall production that they were putting on.

She helped to make costumes, that was all.

Nobody in their new town knew who she was. She hadn't been recognized on the street in more years than she could remember.

For a while, when she was much younger, everyone knew her face. Everyone knew what she had done. Everyone would talk about her when they saw her, as though she were still just a girl on a television set, and not a woman who could hear what they were saying when they were standing in the same room with her.

Those days were gone though. Even if people remembered the story, deep in the back of their minds, they had forgotten her face long ago—and she was no longer that same girl. She was older now. She was a wife, and a mother.

She hadn't danced a single step in nearly twenty years.

Looking at her reflection in that dirty old mirror, in a bathroom that needed new tiling and a new bathtub, in a house that had knob-and-tube wiring until just recently, she paused to study the woman that she had become.

SHE DANCED

She had her mother's eyes, which she saw now more than ever before. She was happy about that. She liked the fact that she had something of her mother's, which she would always carry with her, no matter what happened. It wasn't a knickknack or gaudy jewelry. It was a part of her.

She had her father's smile. At least, she thought so. She'd only ever seen it in pictures before, since she never knew the man.

After having children, she couldn't help but think of all of the people who had gone into the making of her. Not just her physical body, but the person she was.

She was just one person, but she carried them all with her. Even those who were dead.

"Mom!" she heard Sean call from somewhere in the house. "Where's my glove?!"

She closed her eyes and took a deep breath. As she let it out, she yelled back, "Check the kitchen counter!"

The glove would be there, of course, because she had told him a thousand times to keep his dirty old baseball glove away from the kitchen where she had to cook their food.

She had told her boys not to run in the house, but they did it anyway. She had told them not to wrestle with each other inside, but they kept on breaking her porcelain figurines just the same. She told them to be home before dark, but they rarely ever were.

Of course, she would punish them and tell them that they had to follow the rules. She would take away their toys when they misbehaved, or send them to bed without dinner, but she rarely ever felt angry about any of it.

They were children, doing what children were meant to do. Though she would never admit this to them, Maureen enjoyed the sound of their chaos.

When she watched her boys on stage, performing in their little show together, she grinned from ear to ear. Neither one of them could deliver a scripted punchline to save his life, and only Ian had any talent as a singer, but this wasn't the world that she had grown up in. Neither of her kids would be pushed harder and harder, until they learned to do better. Neither one of them would be dragged to auditions and face that rejection time and time again.

They were children. Just children, and the most beautiful things that she had ever set her eyes on.

She walked out of that old bathroom, and made her way through the house. It was just starting to show signs of being hers. Colors that she had chosen. Floors that she had restored.

On the coat rack near the front door, there was a patchwork jacket that she had made herself. She had learned to can her own fruits, and make her own soups. She knew how to bake. She could crochet. She even knew how to set a bone, in theory. She had never tested that skill out though. She'd only learned it because she was curious, about that and so much more.

Maureen was far from being the best at any of these new skills. In fact, she only wore that jacket around her own yard,

SHE DANCED

because she refused to allow all those countless hours to have been wasted.

She just liked trying. Even when she failed.

As she walked out of her house and onto the porch, she could see her boys playing in the front yard, tossing a baseball to each other and racing around as though they'd eaten far more sugar than she had given them permission to eat.

When Ian dropped the baseball and moved to pick it up, he did so by hopping forward on one foot and stretching down in the most awkward way possible. He then threw the ball to his brother, allowing the momentum of that throw to send him into a spin, which promptly landed him on his butt.

Maureen chuckled at the boy as she walked to the front steps and sat down beside Bill, who was also watching the boys play, while petting their puppy, Harvey.

"He gets that from you," Bill said to her.

"You have no idea," she replied.

A cool breeze blew past them, and Maureen closed her eyes, allowing that breeze to wash over her face.

Birds were singing nearby. Bill had some burgers cooking on the grill. He stood and walked to the grill, and Maureen watched him limp as he went.

It had been years since the accident, but she could still remember that night as though it were yesterday. She remembered feeling so scared that she couldn't breathe.

All the worst things seemed to happen to her in the middle of the night. Every time a phone rang after ten o'clock, it made her nervous.

They wouldn't have been on that porch if that accident hadn't happened. Bill was making more money now than he ever would have as a policeman. It wasn't the job he'd always dreamed of, but it allowed them to have days like this.

Quiet. Beautiful.

There were a million things that needed to be done. Errands that needed to be run, and supplies that they needed to pick up from the hardware store before Bill left for a business trip on Tuesday. Maureen needed to figure out where a mouse was getting in, and try to patch whatever hole it was using.

It was a futile task. The house was full of holes, and they would undoubtedly have mice rummaging through their kitchen until they were done fixing the place up. Even then, she wasn't sure that they could keep the pests away.

She was considering getting a cat or two, but she'd never been much of a cat person, so she was resisting the idea of it. Dirty baseball gloves on her counters were bad enough. Dirty paws that had been digging through litter boxes were more than she would be able to tolerate.

Bill flipped the burgers, and stood back to watch them cook. By spring, they would be able to move the grill and the picnic table to the back of the house. Right now, that area was littered with broken glass, rusty nails and rotted wood.

SHE DANCED

This moment was unique. It was a way of life that would come and go, and they would probably never think about it again. Maureen knew that, and she tried her best to create a lasting memory of that moment, because it deserved to be one, but she knew that life would go on. The quiet days were usually the first to be forgotten.

"We should get chickens," Bill said, looking toward the side of the house, where there was a large patch of unused land. He then turned to Maureen, to get her opinion.

"We should," Maureen agreed. "We do eat a lot of eggs."

"What about a goat?" Bill asked.

"Who wouldn't love to have a goat?" she shrugged.

He smiled at her, and took a sip of beer.

Harvey was playing with a piece of old rope by her feet. The boys were trying their best to make up a game of baseball with just the two of them and no field. The air smelled like hamburgers.

As they ate their dinner outside that night, the gentle breeze continued to blow. As the sun went down, Maureen began to feel the first hints of a cold front in that breeze. The sky was clear above them, but she could see clouds in the distance.

After dark, they sat on the covered porch and watched the rain. The boys were listening to drops of water fall onto an old, overturned bucket. In the sound of those drips, they heard music, and they began to sing songs to that beat.

Maureen closed her eyes and listened. Somewhere in the back of her mind, she remembered sitting in the corner of a sound stage, listening to children rehearse songs for the show.

It was a lifetime ago, but for just a fraction of a second, she felt as though she were back there again.

She took a deep breath, and opened her eyes. That other life slipped back into the past where it belonged.

She knew that by morning, there would be chaos once again. The kids would be fighting, the puppy would poop all over the floor. Bill would stub his toe and brood about it. She would forget the secret to getting a hot shower in that house, just as she always did.

She knew that the peace of that day would be lost in the shuffle of life, but she absorbed what she could of that day, while she still had it.

Her life wasn't perfect. There was fighting, and pain and struggle, just as any life had. This was *her* life, however. This was what she had dreamed of when she was a child, and the beauty of that life was not lost on her.

It had taken her a long time to get to this point. She had let people down, and she had spent years feeling guilty about it. She had left everything she had ever known behind, and she started from scratch. She had experienced so much pain and sadness, but this was the light at the end of her tunnel. This was what it had all been building to.

SHE DANCED

How funny it was to think that the only reason she had any of it was because she danced.

∞

As the rest of the season went on, Maureen and Mick became more and more comfortable working together. They spent time together in their off hours, playing stupid games or going to the movies. They attempted to get dinner at a restaurant once, but there was one young girl who just stared at them through their whole meal. She never said anything. She just watched them eat.

From that point on, they would eat their meals in one of their homes, or in some secluded area. Mick kept teaching Maureen new dance steps, and Maureen would make up silly songs to go along with those dances.

On the show, they danced together, but not in the same way that Annie and Ollie danced. While the other two were polished to perfection, given beautiful numbers perform, Mike and Maureen were more of a comedic pairing, with Mick as the straight man to Maureen's goofy comedy.

Maureen liked to think of them as teenaged George and Gracie, and the act worked well for them. They loved making the audience laugh, because it made them laugh too.

At the end of that season, it was announced that Annie's role would be reduced going forward. She was going off to make

TV shows and movies, and while she would pop in from time to time, she would not be in every episode.

Maureen didn't immediately think of this news in terms of her own job. She was just happy for her friend to be headed off for bigger and better things.

When work began on that first season without Annie, it quickly became clear that with their old headlining act out of the picture, the producers would be filling that void with Mike and Maureen routines.

The comedy remained, but the workload increased. Now the pair was being written into multiple sketches, while also being given song and dance numbers to perform each week.

As the season went on, more and more people began to recognize the two of them on the streets, but Maureen and Mick didn't take any of that too seriously. To them, it was all just a big game. The work was a challenge, and they were trying to one-up each other as they went, each trying to push the other just a little bit harder.

In reality, they were tired. Toward the end of the season, both of them were ready for a nice long vacation, but they kept pushing each other, daring each other to be the first to crumble, and in doing so, they kept each other standing.

The rumors were beginning to spread about them. Not romantic rumors—those had been going around since the start—but rumors of sitcom deals and big screen adventures.

SHE DANCED

They tried their best to ignore those rumors, and leave the business decisions to the adults who were running their lives. They just wanted to keep their heads down and try to enjoy what was right in front of them.

"It's silly," Mick told her one day. "You and me, off to star on our own show."

"Is it?" she asked.

"We're not famous or anything. Why give it to us?"

"We're a little famous."

"Not really. And what will we do on our own show? Play high school kids? I've never even been in a high school."

"We could solve mysteries, like Nancy Drew."

"Great. George and Gracie solving mysteries."

"I'd watch that."

"I sure wouldn't."

Maureen laughed at him. The idea was silly. Neither one of them thought of themselves as big stars. Maureen didn't want to allow her mind to wander in that direction. It was too big. It made her stomach churn.

They ended the season by having a small party at that hidden campsite with some of the other kids from the show. Ollie was trying to get his new partner to kiss him, but it wasn't working, which made everyone laugh.

There was more singing and dancing, and this time Maureen danced too.

The fact that any of them wanted to spend time together without trying to sabotage each other or strangle anyone made them unusual, Maureen had come to learn. On other shows, everyone was trying to be the star, and they'd do just about anything to get it.

As they sat around the campfire, she wondered if those other kids might really be plotting her demise. She wondered if she were just naive to think otherwise, or blind to it all because she and Mick tended to keep to themselves.

It didn't seem like it though. She liked those other kids, and they seemed to like her too. It was fun, spending time with them in their off hours, without any rehearsals to think about, or call times to keep in mind.

In that moment, she felt like a kid. A real kid.

Their vacation went on, and the rumors of new shows continued. Maureen was also hearing that the network wanted to expand the show, from weekly to daily. The thought of it made her head spin, but that plan never materialized.

She and Mick spent a lot of time together during their break, while her parents were at work. They would watch TV during the day, and go to the beach at night, when it was too dark for anyone to notice them there.

They would listen to the radio together, and dance in her backyard.

SHE DANCED

"My cousin's getting married next week," Mick told her one day, while they were lounging in the sun. "My brother and I have to drive up for the wedding."

"That sounds fun," Maureen replied.

Mick shrugged and said, "It's five hours away, and all I have to look forward to when I get there is a big family that likes to yell at each other. My Grandma keeps telling me to quit that TV show and start playing sports."

Maureen laughed at that. She said, "I think you'd make a great baseball player."

"I'll be gone for a few days, I guess," Mick said, ignoring her comment.

Maureen sighed and said, "How can I practice dancing without my Mickey here to keep me from falling over?"

He looked over at her for a moment, with a sparkle in his eye and a half smile on his face. It was as though he wanted to say something to her, but he chickened out at the last moment. Instead, he looked around her yard and found a rock the size of his hand.

As he gave that rock to her, he said, "Here. Dance with this."

"A rock?" she laughed.

"You can pretend it's me when I'm gone. You do most of the hard work anyway, so you probably won't even notice the difference."

She laughed again, which made him laugh. She looked the rock over and made a joke about her exciting new dance partner, and the two of them went back to listening to music on the radio.

As the week went on, the two of them continued to spend every day together. Maureen didn't even remember when she had started to assume that they would spend all of their free time with each other. It just happened.

Now she was in the habit of waking up in the morning with Mick on her mind. What movie would they see? What games would they play? Just asking herself such questions brought a smile to her face.

They spent one day at the library, playing a game of silent hide-and-seek in between the stacks, trying to avoid detection by any of the rather stern-looking librarians.

They went swimming with a bunch of the other kids from the show, at a house that belonged to one of those other kids—though Maureen was never sure who.

On the last day that they spent together before Mick left for his trip, they stayed at her house, listening to the radio inside, trying to avoid the summer heat by drinking lemonade and standing in front of fans.

Mick amused himself by singing a song into one of those fans, which made his voice sound like a robot. Maureen tried to pretend that she wasn't amused at all, but the truth was that she'd spent most of the previous night doing the exact same thing.

SHE DANCED

As it got later, Mick picked up Frank's old guitar and started to play along with some of the songs that they were listening to on the radio.

Maureen was making dinner for her parents in the kitchen, since it was getting late and they hadn't come home from work yet.

She was listening to Mick play, and dancing along as she mixed up a salad.

Then he turned off the radio, but kept playing the guitar.

"Hey, wanna hear something that I've been practicing?" he asked her.

"Sure," she said, still giving most of her attention to the work that she was doing.

Mick started to play a more upbeat song as he watched her work. She knew the song. It was *I Want You To Be My Girl*, by Frankie Lymon and the Teenagers.

It was a great song, and Maureen couldn't help but dance as she put a meatloaf in the oven, and started to chop up some potatoes.

The way he sang it was different than she'd heard before though. It was less refined. More raw, as one of her vocal coaches would have put it. As though Mick weren't *performing* the song, he was just allowing that song to flow out of him.

When he was done with the song, he fell silent. She looked back at him and saw that he was waiting for her to react in some way.

"That was beautiful, Mickey," she said, meaning it with all her heart. "But I don't think they'll let you use that one on the show."

"It's not for the show," he replied, with an oddly serious expression on his face.

She didn't get it. She had no idea what he was talking about.

"Are you planning to release a record?" she asked. "Because I think you could."

He looked puzzled for a moment, as though he were trying to comprehend what she was talking about.

Then he flashed that smile that won him a role on their show, and shook his head. He put the guitar down and took a deep breath.

"Thanks," he said to her.

"I really think you could do it," she insisted. "You'd be a huge success too!"

"You're my best friend, you know that?" he asked. Then he shook his head again and told her, "I should get going. I have to leave in the morning and I still haven't packed."

"Okay," she said, turning back to her work. "Have a good time!"

"I'll try. But don't worry, I won't dance with anyone else."

"You better not!" she laughed.

Then he was gone.

Over the next few days, Maureen was left on her own for the first time in what seemed like ages. She would still wake up thinking about what she and Mick should do that day, and then she would remember that Mick wouldn't be home until Sunday.

Being alone was boring. She wished that she could go to work, but there was nothing for her to do at the studio. She was tempted to go out for food or a movie, but the thought of being recognized when she was all by herself made her nervous.

While he was gone, Maureen thought about Mick. She wondered what the future would hold for the both of them. How long could they stay on a TV show that was designed for kids? How long could they keep their act together once they left that show?

Annie and Ollie didn't stay together, and both of them were so talented.

What if Mick really did decide to release a music record? What if he went on tour and became a big success? Where would that leave her? She didn't sing rock and roll.

She didn't like thinking about the future. She was reaching an age where adult decisions would have to be made, and who she became would be the person she was for life.

Kids her age were making big plans for their futures, but Maureen didn't know where to begin. So many of those other kids were dreaming of becoming stars. She'd always dreamed of becoming those other kids.

What if her parents and the men at the studio really did want her to be a big movie star? What if she spent the rest of her life pretending to be other people? Could she do it?

The question of her future kept her up at night. She was seventeen years old now, and she knew that she needed to start making those decisions for herself, but she'd never been good at that.

She wished that Mick would hurry back. He always made things seem so much simpler—especially dancing.

She had been trying to practice her dancing while he was gone, but it was useless. Without him there to catch her, she stumbled and fell. Her brain felt cluttered. Her feet felt like cement blocks. She was a wreck, and the sooner he came home, the better.

It was Saturday night, and Maureen's parents were both home. They'd spent the evening together, watching television and playing card games.

It was a quiet night. A good night. Maureen was trying to fit as many of those quiet nights in as she possibly could, because work would be starting up again soon. Once that happened, she wouldn't be able to rest for months.

After she brushed her teeth and climbed into bed, Maureen's brain raced with chaotic thoughts of music and dance steps. She recalled the sound of Mick singing *I Want You To Be My Girl*, and she tried to imagine herself dancing to it, but even in her head, she stumbled.

The chaos of her thoughts kept her tossing and turning for hours that night, but eventually Maureen fell asleep.

SHE DANCED

It was a deep sleep. The kind of sleep that was hard to pull out of once she was in it.

She heard the telephone ring in the other room, but the sound of it only woke her enough to know that she couldn't drag herself out of bed to answer it.

It rang again, and she wanted to get up, but her body was too heavy.

She heard Frank answer the phone, and she heard him talking to someone on the other end after that. The longer he spoke on the phone, the more she began to drift back into her deep sleep.

Then her bedroom light went on. She could see the light through her eyelids, but she couldn't bring herself to move.

"I can't," she heard her mother say, and then she heard footsteps.

She could hear her mother crying. Why was she crying?

Maureen felt the weight of someone sit down on the side of her bed, and then a hand nudged her shoulder.

"Maureen," Frank whispered. "Sweetie, I need to you to wake up."

Maureen managed a groan, but that was about it.

He shook her a little bit harder, and said, "Maureen, you need to wake up right now."

She opened her eyes. The light was blinding and her head was still lost in a fog of needing more sleep, but she was looking at Frank, not understanding why he was there.

Frank bit on his lip and took a deep breath, trying to find the right words to say what he needed to say. Then he tilted his head, as though he were trying to get on the same level as her, since she was still lying down.

"Arthur just called," Frank said.

Maureen couldn't figure out why Arthur would be calling. Was she late for work? No. They hadn't started work yet.

"He wanted to let us know, before we heard it somewhere else. He's been getting calls from reporters who…" Frank stopped himself, realizing that none of what he was saying made sense to Maureen, and none of it even mattered.

He took another deep breath.

"Frank? What's happening?" Maureen said, just barely able to form the words now.

He looked her squarely in the eyes and said, "Sweetie… There was an accident tonight. A horrible accident, and Mick was…"

"Mick?" Maureen asked, suddenly feeling more awake.

Frank swallowed hard and finished, "Mick is dead, sweetie. He died in the accident."

There was silence for a moment, as Frank allowed those words to sink in. Except, they didn't sink in. Maureen didn't understand them.

She shook her head and smiled, saying, "No, that's not right. Mick isn't even in town. He's away, at a wedding."

"His car was hit by a man who ran through a red light," Frank told her.

SHE DANCED

"He doesn't have a car. He doesn't drive. It wasn't Mick."

"His brother was driving," Frank pressed. "They decided to drive overnight and get home early. Their car was hit, and… Maureen, I need for you to understand what I'm telling you. Mick is dead."

Maureen sat up in her bed. She was fully awake now, but she didn't feel awake. The world felt like it was humming around her, and when she got out of her bed, she didn't feel herself walking. It was as though she were floating from one spot to the next.

She knew the words that Frank had used, and she knew how those words fit together into sentences, but it didn't make sense to her.

Maureen walked out of her bedroom and into the hallway. She saw her mother standing at the far end, holding a hand over her mouth. Her mother was staring at her, waiting to see what Maureen would do next.

"Maureen," her mother whispered.

"Mick is dead," Maureen said to her mother, starting the sentence quietly, but ending it in sobs.

She fell onto the floor, unable to stop the tears once they had started.

∞

It was September, 1960.

The funeral had come and gone. The reporters had stopped trying to get a picture of Maureen with big, puffy eyes. Life was going on for most people, as though nothing had changed.

Work had already started on the show, but Maureen hadn't been back there yet. The idea of walking onto that studio lot and stepping onto that stage felt wrong to her. Everything felt wrong. Ever since Mick died, she'd felt as though she were hovering just above her body, watching everything happen around her.

In one desperate frenzy, Maureen had run into her backyard to find the rock that Mick had given her on one of their last days together.

'You can pretend it's me when I'm gone,' he'd told her.

For some reason, she felt as though holding that rock would make her feel closer to him, and might take away some of the hurt that she felt every moment of every day.

The rock didn't help her, and yet she couldn't manage to throw it away either. She kept on her bedside table, and stared at it before she went to sleep at night, trying to recall every second of every day that they'd spent together.

She remembered the look that he'd given her after singing that song. She had been too busy to give it much thought at the time, but now she wished that she could ask him what he was so amused by.

SHE DANCED

After some time, her mother sat down beside Maureen and told her that she needed to get out of the house. She needed to be around people, and she needed to get back to work.

Work felt stupid to her. It had always felt stupid to her, except when Mick was there, but Maureen didn't argue with her mother. She didn't care enough about where she was, because the hollow feeling inside of her was sure to be with her, no matter where she went.

And so, she went to work. The show was preparing for the new season to begin. Obviously, they'd had to scramble to replace all of the segments that she and Mick were supposed to be in together, so there was nothing for her to do, except sit and watch all of the other people go about their work.

The other kids were bickering with each other. Maureen watched them from her dark, quiet corner. She'd never noticed any of them bickering before, and it seemed strange to her now.

Annie was flying in from England, to perform in the premiere episode of the new season. She had been away, filming a movie, but she'd agreed to come home when the producers called her and asked her to fill some of those empty spaces.

Maureen was there on the day Annie arrived, and she watched as Annie walked onto the stage and gave everyone hugs. She'd missed the funeral, so this was the first time that Maureen had seen her since Mick died.

Over the next couple of hours, she watched Annie speak to the producers and go over their script. Every so often, she would see Annie ask someone on the crew a question, and then glance in Maureen's direction.

When Annie walked over to where Maureen was sitting, Maureen didn't know what to expect. She wasn't feeling up to smiling and pretending to be happy to see Annie, or anyone else.

Annie didn't smile either. She just stood beside Maureen for a few moments, watching everyone else work. Maureen could feel her trying to find words, but what was Annie supposed to say?

"I heard *Tammy* on the radio this morning," Annie finally said. "When I heard it, it reminded me of that night when you sang it by the fire. I didn't know Mick very well that night, but I saw the look in his eye when you were singing. This strange, curious look, as though he'd just discovered something unbelievable."

Maureen looked over at Annie, and she could see Annie playing that night back in her mind. For the first time, she felt as though someone else understood what had happened to the world.

Annie looked at Maureen and put on a sympathetic smile as she said, "I wish someone would look at me that way. Like they really saw me."

She brushed a tear from her eye, and then asked Maureen, "Can I tell you something? Even if it sounds rude, and you don't want to hear it?"

Maureen nodded.

Annie took a moment to consider her words, and then said, "He loved you, from the very first day. You must know that.

SHE DANCED

And the two of you made each other great—better than any of the rest of us. And… Well, I would just hate to see him be the thing that holds you down, that's all. And he would hate that too. Whatever you do, you can't let him become that to you."

After she said that, Annie returned to work, and Maureen thought about what she'd said. She also wondered what the rest of the crew members had told Annie. How many of them were expecting her to fall apart? How many of them thought that she was nothing without Mick?

If she were being honest about it, she also though that she was nothing without him.

She watched rehearsals for the rest of the week. By the end of it, she knew everyone's lines, probably better than they did.

Maureen was trying to figure out a way to become what she had been before. She wanted to find the part of herself that smiled on that stage and made people laugh, but the truth was, none of that mattered to her anymore. How could she pretend for the rest of her life?

This wasn't new. Despite what people might have thought about her, this wasn't something that just happened after Mick died. This was something that had always been there. She had always been the girl who sat by herself and watched everyone else go about their work.

She knew that she would have to find some way to get through it. She would have to get back to putting on a show for people. She just didn't know how to do that by herself.

Show day arrived. The big premiere episode of the new season, and everyone was trying their best to pull together and make this show the very best that it could be.

There was chaos, and drama. Stress was high.

There had been gossip about the show in the press, but Maureen hadn't been paying attention to any of that. There were arguments between producers and the network. There was some level of anger in the air, but Maureen hadn't cared enough to ask about it, and nobody felt a need to bring it to her.

It was nearly showtime, when that tension began to boil over. Kids were running around, trying to pull themselves together before they were expected to perform on live TV, in their fancy costumes and their perfectly-done hair.

One of those kids was Violet. She was wearing a gown which shimmered in the light and gathered around her feet. She was going to be the final act of the night, and the wardrobe department just needed to make one last adjustment to the gown before they went on.

It would be a grand performance. Maureen had seen it a hundred times already.

Violet would have performed a sort of ballet dance, while singing a song about the changing seasons.

That is to say, she would have done the number if she hadn't tripped on the gown and twisted her ankle, just before the show went on the air.

SHE DANCED

Within minutes, the ankle was swelling up. Violet was in a great amount of pain, and they needed to get her to a hospital.

Arthur was trying his best to keep the show together, but he was reaching a breaking point, and Maureen could see that.

Being the professional that she was, she told Arthur, "I know the song."

He turned to her and looked at her as though he hadn't even realized that she was there until that moment.

"I don't know the dance, but I know the song. I can sing it," she said.

Arthur didn't need to think very hard about this decision, since he would have no closing act without her.

Once it was agreed upon, Maureen was rushed through the process of hair and makeup. She was put into one of her old costumes, since the wardrobe people didn't have time for anything new.

A hundred different moments were coming together now, though nobody could see fate unfolding before them.

At the end of the show, Maureen took the stage.

She stood there, by herself for the first time in years, under the spotlight.

The image of herself on television came back to her in that moment, looking stupid as she stood there and sang her little song.

She couldn't do that again. She couldn't be the girl she once was. She refused to just stand there and sing.

So, as she began to sing her song, Maureen started to move.

Her song began in springtime, when flowers were in bloom. The promise of all that was to come.

She didn't think about how she was moving as she sang the song. For the first time in her life, she had just let go, and her body was moving for her. It was gliding and spinning.

The song moved into summer, with the sun shining bright and warm. Games played. Fun had.

It was only as she did a bit of hopscotch that Maureen realized that she did know this dance after all, and she smiled at the memory of it.

Then she moved into autumn, when the first cold wind blows leaves to the ground.

She spun, and glided through this dance, because she had done it a thousand times before. She did the dance without him this time, but he was there. She could feel him, just behind the spotlight.

Winter brought the bitter cold, and fires burned inside. Nights are dark and long in the wintertime.

She did it. She dipped, but she didn't fall. She spun, into where his arms should have been, but once again, she stood alone beneath the spotlight.

In that moment, all she could do was try her best not to cry, because the spell was broken. She was once again just the same girl that she had always been.

Then springtime came again.

SHE DANCED

When the song was over, she stood there, waiting. For the longest time, she looked toward the light, but she couldn't see anything. It was too bright.

It was also too quiet. So much so that Maureen had started to wonder if everyone had gone home for the night, when she heard someone yell "Cut! And we're out!"

Then the light went off.

As Maureen's eyes adjusted, the first person she saw was Annie. She was holding onto Ollie, crying into his chest.

Maureen didn't know what had happened, but as she looked from face to face, and person to person, she saw that most of them were crying too. Even the big men who built the sets were trying to hold back tears.

Arthur was standing beside the camera, with wide eyes and a hand over his mouth.

Then someone started to clap, and before she knew it, everyone was clapping and crying, and Maureen still had no idea what was happening.

She didn't know, because she hadn't been paying attention to it.

After Mick's death, the press was going crazy. The story of a child star, dead before his time, was all over the place.

Arthur and the other producers wanted to memorialize Mick when the show came back, but the network refused to allow it. The show was called The Happy Slappy Fun Time Kids Variety

Hour, and the last thing they needed was to drag out the sad publicity that they were getting.

The best they would offer was a series of *best-of* episodes, airing before the show came back. *The Best of Annie and Ollie!* The best songs. The best comedy.

And the week before the show came back, they aired *The Best of Mike and Maureen*.

The ratings went through the roof for that episode, which cut together all of the couple's best routines, and the hour closed by showing their first-ever dance together.

Around the country, viewers laughed and cried together, and newspapers wrote about the tragedy of it all.

The network hated it, but there was nothing else they could do about it.

When Maureen agreed to perform that song during the season's opening episode, it caught everyone off guard—herself included. But Annie was right, and Maureen couldn't allow Mick to become the thing that held her back.

So, she performed, and she danced, and without intending to do it, or knowing what would happen if she did, Maureen memorialized Mick in the closing act of their season premiere.

Everyone in the studio was grieving together, and some of them came to hug Maureen as well.

When the telephone rang, Maureen hardly even noticed it.

Then she heard Arthur yell, "Are you joking?"

The entire place fell silent as they listened to his phone call.

SHE DANCED

"I won't. I won't do that," he said. "You can't…"

Then the call was over, and a stunned Arthur hung up the phone.

He looked up at Maureen, with tears still in his eyes, and in barely a whisper, he informed her, "You're fired."

∞

Marriage. Children. Retirement. Loneliness and loss.

The world changed a lot over the course of Maureen's life, and it continued to change once she was dead.

The year 2020 was a low point for many people. They were feeling more isolated and alone than ever before. The world was falling apart around them, and there was nothing they could do about it.

At the time, new video streaming services were coming online, giving the world access to countless hours of videos that had been locked away for decades.

While in bed one night, a young girl stumbled upon an archive of Happy Slappy Fun Time Kids Variety Hour episodes, and was swept away by the retro fun.

A short time later, the girl posted a photo to her social media, of a girl dancing by herself under a spotlight.

She captioned the photo, *'Me During Lockdown'*.

Though she didn't expect much from this post, the girl was shocked to see it shared by a Broadway star, and then by millions of other people around the world.

The girl's picture was turned into t-shirts, and the image of that girl dancing was even turned into a mural, on the side of a skyscraper.

The girl's sad, captivating performance drew her audience in, even decades later.

Most didn't know who this girl was, or why she was performing alone. They didn't know what it was about that girl that made her so haunting.

All they knew was that she danced.

Now that you've finished reading this book, please remember to post your review online!

If you'd like to send the author a comment, email him at:

author.kyleandrews@gmail.com

If you enjoyed **She Danced**, be sure to look for these other titles by Kyle Andrews:

STARLETTE

STRANGE FALL

SPIRIT OF CHRISTMAS

The Freedom/Hate Series

FREEDOM/HATE

BLOOD RIGHTS

THE SECRET CITIZEN

BATTLE CRY

OUTBOUND

IF WE FALTER

Made in the USA
Coppell, TX
19 August 2023

20452897R00069